When beginning converges, Infinity diverges

love
aurora
dream
whatsapp
area of fortune
samayra
aurora
tesseract fear
graphs
alpha
island
two brains
mathematics
love
dimensions
happiness
senses aurora
purohit
fear
wormhole
insecurities
neurons
functions

INFINITY
The novella

Mallika Chawla and Abhishek Leela Pandey

A BROKEN TUSK *PRESENTATION*

First published in India by Broken Tusk Publishers
All Rights reserved 2020

Cover Design by ALP Designs

Typeset in Bookman Old Style 11 pts.

Printed at Gagan Printers, Ludhiana

A network of branches was formed which extended to random directions and dimensions. After a while the graphs looked like a tesseract and there was one door made of grayscale wire-mesh. Samayra moved inside the door and its width was infinitely converging towards the other end. Along the width there were wire-mesh windows each containing a three dimensional image of her time with Purohit. She maneuvered across the **infinite** gallery to reach another door with a board which read 'The Equation of Love.'

Guidelines to read this book

This book is the love story of a mathematician with a girl who has fascination towards the Pure and Applied disciplines of Mathematics. It is a novella which talks about the most important events in their life. The other details have deliberately been excluded. The language used in the book is a blend of modern day English and mathematical technicality. For those who do not belong to mathematical background, the authors have given relevant and lucid explanations and footnotes.

The book talks about theorems, axioms and corollaries. The text towards the end of the story would resemble a scientific journal with appropriate graphs and citations.

Let's begin the legend which deserves to be shared with the world!

PS: The multiple usage of text in italics is the fast-forward narration of the story

MYTH vs REALITY

**The humanity is not about what it is
capable of perceiving,
It is about what is out there!**

Prologue

Purohit was born in a small village at the border of present day Uttarakhand and Nepal. His family belonged to royalty but his great grandfather had lost it all when his lands were compromised for a meagre amount during British Raj. As a result his grandfather had to try hard to make ends meet, for the rest of his life. He was a father to six sons and one daughter. His eldest son and Purohit's father was a brilliant man. He had a vision and worked hard for earning a job at the central government. He met a lady and instantly fell for her. The lady was as brilliant as he was, but more privileged and hence, more educated. The family arranged their meeting and as love was easy to comprehend then, they got married.

Three years later, Purohit was born. He and his mother stayed in the village until he was five years old. The village, the simplicity of the surroundings and nature had a profound impact on Purohit. His mother taught him the basics of science and literature until they moved to the city of Dehradun, when his father felt the need of formal education for his son. His father took his wife and son to the city, and kept providing for everyone in his extended family, back village.

Purohit was a gifted mathematician. He was three years old when he found a pattern in the movement of ants, flight of pigeons, growth of trees and nerves on his father's hands. At five, he had developed a geometrical pattern to distinguish in his own ways, the faces which looked beautiful and the ones which didn't. At an age of seven, he made a theorem to calculate the sums of sequential numbers, arithmetic and geometric. By the age of twelve, he had read the Elements by Euclid, Principia by Newton and Divina by Leonardo da Vinci.

His approach to mathematics was considered philosophical by his teachers and friends. Philosophy gives rise to artistic pursuits. This realization made him write a series of poems till the age of nineteen. It happened at an age of twenty two that he started training students for entrance exams which involved mathematics and English language.

Let's halt for a while! Four years after he was born, the other character of this story came into existence; Samayra!

Samayra was born in Chandigarh. Her father was a businessman and the mother was a homemaker. She grew in a disciplined household, which gave ethics and well-being the highest priority. She showed exceptional intelligence in the field of applied mathematics and economics. As a child, she was the favorite of her school teachers for seminars, declamations and quizzes. She was always the first to answer the most complex questions asked in the school. Her delicate frame and soft voice made her look like a kid, even after she grew sixteen. The negative externality of being intelligent and humble, is envy, and she was a victim of that. She was bullied by her classmates. She grew insecure and closed. She made a wall around her, and grew with it. She got so much used to it that 'confusion about human behavior' became her general mindset; and, it worked wonders for her. Give no explanations, and people won't question! Ignorance is bliss, they say!

Purohit was always ignorant of the real world. He never knew if someone was bullying, respecting, loving or hating him, and it worked for him too!

That was all about their backgrounds. This story starts at a point when Purohit had become a renowned mathematician and Samayra, a student at one of the India's top Business Schools.

Mathematics is what made them meet!

So, we begin, here!!

EVENT 1
The Dream

"Once upon a time, there lived a sage, in the deep forests of exploration, somewhere in a **field**[1], made of unknown dimensions. He knew the place well; the flora and fauna, the brooks, the thirsty deer, the iridescent butterflies, the blades of grass flanked by the glowworms in the dark nights of solace. He relished on the juicy fruits and drank by the cascade. He waited for the humanity to arrive to his little beautiful world. Little did he know that the path was chaotic, like a maze, much like his multi-dimensional thoughts! He had to believe he would have to usher them to this path. The path that scientists and mathematicians termed wormholes[2]! "

∞ ∞ ∞

The dreams of yesterday were vivid in his eyes, in full colors and shape. The brook, the blades of grass, the glowworms and the other finer details (with intact geometry) were all in his memory. But he also knew the nuances of everyday world. He realized he had to go to work. He rubbed his eyes as the chaotic curls in his hair intruded them. He looked at the window beside his bed and could see the entire city covered up with smog. The AQI of New Delhi was at an all-time high.

He looked at the watch. He was supposed to take a seminar in a B School at 11 AM. His getting-ready routine just took fifteen minutes, because nothing really changed about his appearance except the fact that he was dressed now. He loved sleeping naked as he believed the skin-

---

[1] *A field is a set on which mathematical operations are performed*
[2] *Wormholes connect one point to another distant point in zero time.*

pores have a mind of their own. His attire was a sweatshirt which remained unmatched to his jeans, as always. He looked one final time at the mirror of his bathroom, the only place he believed people look real.

11 AM, Delhi University

"Mr. Purohit Khantwal is a polymath working in the fields of pure mathematics, quantum mechanics, data structures and surprisingly, poetry. There are patterns in almost everything we do or choose not to do. The patterns of language, market sentiments, economics, politics, history and mathematics! He researches on the patterns which we mostly ignore, and also develops new ones. Today he is here to talk about his latest theorems on mathematics. The Fashion of Mathematics Inc. in association with Mr. Khantwal is launching a certification course, which would be of great help to the future managers of our college. We welcome him on the stage!" The anchor declared.

Purohit walked to the stage and looked around the auditorium. A highly ambitious and determined group of students were waiting for a revelation. He sensed the urgency and impatience. Music played in his mind, probably jazz, or opera. He jumped over the group of students and glided his way through the ends of auditorium and found a permanent place to stay in one of the corners, where he could sense the emotion of the audience.

Not fruitful, he thought!

He was the kind of person who followed vibes, and the vibes in the auditorium had communicated to him that the audience was passive.

Nonetheless, he picked up the microphone.

"The functions of reality are objective to our senses! Physical Senses! The five senses are not the organs of exploration, but a limitation of humans."

His trail of thoughts got disrupted by a very strong presence of a wave. He tried to look for the source, but in vain.

"When we talk about the physical structures, for example, beauty, we transgress to the established notions of objective reality, which changes with regions and nationalities. Do we actually have a standard pattern for knowing beauty from ugliness, good from bad, the rigidity of a stone from the stone-hearted, like we know white from black? Science says black and white are just sensations and they don't have an objective reality. It is what all of us believe in, as a highly organized assembly of tissues usually called as humans. It is this fluidity of concepts which I always wanted to address, if..."

The wave was strong and he felt weak in knees, which was a rarity in his case.

"If that makes sense to you," he said and waited for the audience to acknowledge. He had mastered the art over years to get connected to the audience by waiting for their absorption time, but this time it was different. Why would a management graduate need that kind of information? He had to sound relevant.

"The emotions of market can be termed as objective reality as there is no fundamental way of practicing finance as a discipline. The greatest finance guys were dependent on their instincts and common sense. Let's consider Warren Buffet! What do you know about him?"

"He is one of the greatest guys in finance the world has ever seen," a young man in the front row said.

"He is the world's richest investor," a girl said.

"Well! He is such an intelligent investor that he has still got 1.28 billion dollars in his firm Berkshire Hathway but no options to invest. That is the kind of success we should aim at. Having said that, I have devised statistical functions which take into consideration at least thousand variables, including exclusions like empathy, corruption and religion," Purohit counted on his fingers.

The session continued for another half an hour. Purohit introduced his certification program and the whole crowd cheered. The anchor took hold of the stage and presented him a memento, followed by a speech by the dean of the college.

12 Noon

The students gathered around him, praising and interacting, and like a routine, he found himself granting everyone with an acknowledging nod in the same monotony. Of course, he was preoccupied! What his brain was doing would be insanity in general consensus, but for him it was the only way of perceiving things (including living ones). He was busy allotting geometrical design to everyone. In his reality, people looked like meshes and matrices of uncountable thread-like structures. This was his style of analysis and observation.

But after this phase got over, he continued with the 'social version' of him.

He did not like being pretentious, but he had to do this to make people not dislike him.

When the social 'him' was trying hard to come out of the zone of geometrical figures, something suddenly hurled him back. This zone switching had never been this fast. It had to be done because he came across the queerest figure he had seen or will ever see. This was pure amazement.

The entire hallway looked like an organized arrangement of grayscale cuboids and cubes with human-meshes wandering around, but one particular figure had an orange tinge, something he had never witnessed before.

The tinge was her. In the world of intelligible figures fitting one scale or another, she was an infinitely diverged orange tinge beyond perception and measurements. The units to contain her were yet to be discovered, the dimension to which she belonged to, was yet to be demystified, but he could not see her. Before he could come out of his geometrical sight-seeing, she was gone. He took the incident as a figment of his own hallucination and applauded his creativity. He marked the day as the day of an unprecedented meeting of his creativity with something beyond senses and dimensions humans are aware of.

2 AM

The known universe comprises of four types of forces. After Big Bang happened, three dimensions were formed, and a fourth dimension[3] was formed too, but it was temporal. The organs of perception were three dimensional so humans couldn't comprehend 'time'. They rather confused it to be a definite truth. It took humanity close to million years to develop quantum mechanics and think of time as relative. Recent searches have concluded that there are at least thirty nine dimensions which behave simultaneously. Every action, physical or non-physical has an explanation if all the dimensions are considered.

'Solitude' is a vague term. People consider solitude to be a physical phenomenon, but it needs a great deal of courage and sensibility to understand that there are non-physical presences as well. Humans feel uneasy when they feel a presence which can't be seen or touched.

Alas! They are bound by their physical bodies.

Purohit woke up as if nudged by someone. He saw the blue LED still shining over his head, but this time it had a personality of its own. In a half-awake state, he felt the bulb wanted to talk to him. He looked beyond the bulb to analyze the reason for his uneasiness, but the source was inside his blanket. It nudged again.

INFINITY started following you…
The Instagram notification read.

∞ ∞ ∞

---

[3] *Time is considered to be the fourth dimension. It prevents all the events to happen at once.*

EVENT 2
Samayra
(Same day as Event 1)

It was the same lentils being served for the third time this week at Samayra's hostel. For the consumers, it was a punishment, but for the cook it was a delight. The cook had probably robbed an island full of lentils and didn't want to sell it off, as he was too attached with it. So he cooked it instead, every other day by manifesting his love and cherishing the fact that he had been the victor of the island.

After dinner, as it was the ritual amongst hostellers to talk about their day and rather flaunt about all they had been doing, girls flocked and began the procession. As in a congregation, they came, performed their service and went back to their respective spots.

Samayra kept watching and listening to them. She was an atheist in this world of theists. She preferred talking to her own self about the day. She went back to her room. She lived her nights the way others lived the onset of their days. The only difference being, they recalled the dreams they had and she recalled the day she had.

Someone knocked! It was Maya, her neighbor who stopped by, to get some notes. They were in the same college, doing same course. While Samayra was looking around for the notes, Maya couldn't help but notice how fastidious Samayra was. The books were arranged according to size and thickness. From nail paints to lipsticks, everything was aligned in a continuum.

The topic that followed the small talk was of the seminar. Maya's facial and verbal expressions betrayed her dislike for Purohit. After all, he did not look like the mathematicians she had seen in school textbooks.

"How did you like that nerd?" Maya jumped on a couch.

"He had interesting points to make," Samayra mumbled, while searching for the notes.

"I didn't understand a word." Maya said and smiled.

"I liked the way that man sees mathematics. I have not seen anyone doing that, including my teachers at school. They tried really hard to make me hate that subject."

"In my case, they succeeded!" Maya chuckled.

"Did you notice the way he was looking at the walls and pillars, as if he was calculating something?"

"I was noticing his eyes only. They were intense," Maya exclaimed.

Samayra rolled her eyes.

"What?" Maya smiled.

"He sounded like an old man sitting inside the body of a young man," Samayra was surprised at how vividly she remembered everything about him, for she had never been the observant type. Unlike her vague dreams, the picture of him giving the seminar was a high-definition DSLR clicked Polaroid.

"Yes, he looked good!" That was all Maya could say.

"Let's google him out!" Samayra opened her laptop.

Purohit Khantwal is a mathematician and poet from India. He has created seven theorems under his research paper. He has actively been associated with organizations pertaining to mathematical modelling, data science, training, and social work.

Samayra was already fascinated by mathematics, and Purohit had made a mark in her mind. She searched more about him, and reached his Instagram handle. There were pictures of him taking seminars, mathematical quotes and poems. She kept on exploring the profile.

She hit the 'follow' tab. It was 2 AM. She called it a night!

∞ ∞ ∞

EVENT 3
The First Call

With every hair on his stubble that got shaved and fell on the floor, he felt beads of perspiration flowing from his neck to the towel tied on his waist, and vanishing. The beads slowly transformed into downy flakes rendering him a tickle. As the day clears the foggy dawn, the sunrise melted the flakes; like the warm touch of a lover's hand caressing all over from top to bottom and then top again. Purohit had a vivid and graphic imagination. That's why; probably he could feel things which few did.

This lovemaking was snapped with the notification of his mobile. His new follower was pressing 'like' on all of his pictures, second by second. He was tempted to reciprocate. He came across the picture from yesterday on the follower's Instagram profile. He saw himself on the stage and her on the seventh row and seventh column of the auditorium. He thought about the number seven, mysterious according to numerology, and prominent everywhere else, from the oceans to the continents to the days in a week and wonders of the world. Keeping the phone aside he continued the love making but this time with his real love- Coffee!

He received a call from an unknown number. The caller wanted to know when he will be starting with the certification program. He felt it was the same person who had been going through his social media account. He thought the possibility of him being right was worth the shot so he questioned, "Are you infinity?"

"Yes, I am Infinity. I mean I am not Infinity but the username name is. My name is Samayra."

"That's a nice name", Purohit paused, thought for a while and continued, "The program will be starting soon."

"How can I get enrolled in it?"

"By a written test, followed by an interview!"

"Would it be a lot of mathematics?" She laughed.

"A bit of it!"

"What are the prerequisites?"

"Nothing but a beautiful brain!"

Beautiful brain! The words resonated in Samayra's ears for a while. That was crazy! Being a mathematician can make a person weird, being a poet weirder, but being both, weirdest.

"When can I give the test?"

"Tomorrow!"

"At what time and where?"

"10 AM in my office."

"Sure, I will see you there!"

$$\infty \ \infty \ \infty$$

EVENT 4
Coffee

Samayra reached Purohit Consults at 10 AM as decided. The inside of the office had an upbeat trendy feel. The design of the walls looked like lifted directly from the Old Hollywood Classics. The vintage etching on the glass looked like a high-end design studio. The false ceiling had organic patterns and small fairy-lights to increase the contrast. On the extreme right, a girl was sitting at the reception.

"Hello Madam," she greeted.

"I want to meet Mr. Khantwal." Samayra arranged her brown leather handbag.

"Are you Samayra?"

"Yes!"

"I will call him up," the receptionist took out her phone. Samayra noticed a shelf where Purohit's books were displayed. They ranged from calculus and ring theory to topology. One was poetry. She picked it up, and opened a random page. The poem was called 'sweetheart', which read like this:

What conceal'th he

In the bosom wide

The shadow o'realms

Deep oceans tide,

Calm on persona, scarred eyebrow

Conceal'th the earthy innocence,

Plumping steadfast, the lost pride

What maketh the world o' dreams

"Screams and Creams"

Or, "Screams or Creams"

And thusly devastated, lied he,

In the bed o' dreams,

The bed o' screams

Until one fine morn'

He saw the dew, stark

Covering the skin o' dreams

Many a nights, scorn'th he

Until one fine morn'

He seeketh she

O what plight can't be remov'th

As we see, as we be

He picked up his sweetheart

In his strong arms,

Roll'th on sea, cajol'th the storms

In the hopes of strength, found she,

Ris'th he, Ris'th she

Ris'th them

What conceal'th he?

Oh, sweetheart thee!!

She imagined the places and situations in the poem. Her trail of thoughts broke when the receptionist called, out loud.

"He would take some time to come but you can visit his place, if you want."

"Where is he?"

"He stays upstairs!"

"That will be easy to find," Samayra smiled.

"Yeah, busy man!" the receptionist smiled back.

Purohit's apartment had an entry resembling a cave. It was made with stone and wood. Had it not been Delhi, it would have looked like the abode of a majestic animal, a lion, a tiger, a dragon, a unicorn, a hobbit, may be!

She ringed the bell.

'Come in," It was Purohit's voice.

Samayra entered the studio apartment and located Purohit on the other end. He had a mug in his hands with the imprint of a mathematical equation.

$$e^{i\pi} + 1 = 0$$

"It is the most beautiful equation known to mankind," Purohit said and walked to her. She noticed him carefully. He had an intense and moist pair of eyes. His stance was alarming and confident. He was clad in black shirt and gray trousers. The shoes were still to be worn and a black tie was lying on the couch.

"Hello, I am Samayra," she extended her hands. Purohit looked at thin yet firm fingers of Samayra.

"What are you calculating?" Samayra asked.

"Ah! Nothing!" He smiled and they shook hands.

"You have an unconventional but nice house," she looked around.

"Thanks! Would you like some coffee?" He offered her the cup.

"You were telling about the equation!" Her love for mathematics overpowered the smell of coffee. "This equation encompasses all the mathematical functions known to mankind. It is commonly known as God's equation. It was developed by Euler. It governs the Universe and defines the human soul."

"How?" Samayra got interested.

"I will tell, but before that smell this thing," he came closer. The aroma of finest coffee beans and his perfume inundated her nostrils.

"Davidoff, Cool Water?" Samayra exclaimed.

"Yes!"

"I cannot imagine a nerd for having a taste for perfumes." She immediately realized she should not have said that.

"It is gifted." Purohit said looking closely at Samayra. Her wafer thin lips, tiny pointed nose and broad forehead were so perfect. Her neck was flanked with a chiseled collarbone. He couldn't help but notice through her sleeveless top that her arms were long and slender. Her fair skin contrasted with tiny veins at the wrist.

"It smells so nice," her eyes shone.

"I pick my coffee from finest stores," he laughed. She looked at his unkempt wavy hair curling at his earlobes. His clean-shaven face was glowing with calmness and wisdom. She realized that she was noticing too much of him and tried to deviate.

"I read your poem, the sweetheart. It was beautiful."

"I wrote it for my ex-girlfriend."

"Oh, you had a girlfriend!"

"Why not?"

"I talk a lot, sorry," she made a face, which looked cute to Purohit. His masculine notions of romance came to the fore.

"You talk alright. No one has actually talked to me from a long time," Purohit sipped on his coffee.

"Still, I should talk sense!" Samayra bent her lips.

"I am starting the course next week. Till then you can unofficially start with me," he offered.

"But you are a busy man!" She rolled her eyes.

"Not much," Purohit checked out his appointments on phone.

"But, won't you test if I deserve to be a part of this?"

"You already have mathematical acumen. You are infinity." He tried to crack a joke.

"I am embarrassed." She twisted her lips sideways, and suddenly realized she is being watched.

"You are like a kid."

"I want to be one, always."

Purohit felt the urge to communicate to her. He felt something was common between them.

"I was never a kid," Purohit said and tried to copy her lip-twisting.

"But you are a copycat!"

They both laughed. After a while, Purohit stopped and looked at Samayra who was still laughing, with left hand on her mouth. The background blurred for him and his inquisitive eyes observed every contour on her face.

"I think I should leave now," Samayra said.

"Well, I am free this week and you can drop by, anytime."

Samayra acknowledged and left.

That was the day when it started, but only in the mind of Purohit. Samayra was a friendly, but very cautious person. She knew the extremes of her interaction, but more than that, she considered Purohit to be a mentor. That was the curse Purohit was born with. He became a trainer at an age when everyone else was studying.

∞ ∞ ∞

EVENT 5
The Workshop

A week later, it was time for the first day of the workshop. He did not bother to waste time in ice-breaking session. The class had just the optimum number of students, neither too many nor too few. Purohit devoted equal attention to all the students but one. Like a worker comes back after a long tiring day and finds comfort under the roof of his home, his eyes kept coming back to Samayra who was busy jotting down whatever he said in her notes.

As soon as the class got over, Samayra rushed back. Purohit could not decide whether he should feel regretful for not trying to stop her and start a conversation, or feel like an idiot for longing for someone like this.

From first to fourth session, nothing changed much except the topics he taught in the workshop. Every night lying on his bed, he felt his mind was nothing but a pendulum oscillating between the two extreme questions- 'Why did she not stop?' and 'Why would she stop?'

He finally realized it was stupid of him to nurture any such feelings for any student. He consciously tried not to think of her, or see her, or talk to her!

Samayra failed to notice how he had been making efforts for her, but she certainly noticed when he was trying to be away from her on the fifth day. She took it as a student-teacher issue. As she had always been a teachers' favorite student, she concluded the issue demanded immediate resolution.

To fathom the seriousness and reason of the issue, she stayed back after the sixth class on the ground of some mathematical queries.

Purohit was elated when she asked whether he was free to take her doubts. He surrendered the whole boycott agenda without any thought.

Samayra realized the conflict was just a result of her over-thinking and Purohit realized thinking and love can't go hand in hand.

"Are you alright?" Samayra asked.

"Yes, why?" Purohit tried to shift his gaze towards her notebook.

"You are behaving strange."

"The vector field can be integrated in majority of the cases," Purohit made a circle on one of the graphs she had plotted.

"Really?" Samayra was interrogative. Purohit was confused about which part of the conversation she was asking about. Was it his behavior or the vector field? The next statement by Samayra shocked him to the core.

"Your behavior is an exception if it is represented as a vector field," Samayra chuckled.

"I think mathematics fails when it comes to expression of human behavior," Purohit urged.

"I thought you can do it," Samayra said and continued, "That is what you are meant for; to quantify the unquantifiable!"

Men are chaotic, but women maintain the order.

That evening Purohit got nostalgic and pulled out his ex-girlfriend's picture. The flashes of past ran through his mind. They had planned on being together, but his way of doing things freaked her out. He always tried to find a mathematically verifiable reason for everything. It took a message from Samayra the same night for him to realise that it wasn't mathematics that was responsible for his break-up, but the difference in thought-processes. This is why two humans remain together throughout life. He concluded that mathematics was not just a subject, but a way of living. It was a soft skill acquired by few. Samayra had that!

Samayra was hope for him; a hope that his intelligence was not a curse that distanced him from other humans and deprived him of common human emotions; a hope that there was love somewhere for him too. She was the bridge that could connect him to the rest of the world. She could comprehend both the sides- him as well as the world.

This new-found meaning of life developed in him, determination to go beyond the apparent boundaries of human thought.

The mathematician couldn't believe in anything without quantification. He resolved to quantify his feelings for Samayra and for the reference of generations to come. The minor reason behind resolution was his urge to document. The major reason was to make feelings communicable between him and her.

He made it a point that he would never lose her, whatever it takes!

∞ ∞ ∞

EVENT 6
Area of Fortune

7 PM
Purohit's residence

"So what do you think?" Purohit handed over a diagram to Samayra.

The last days of workshop were spent in them getting close over mathematical and philosophical insights. They had decided to work together on a theory which would take into consideration quantum mechanics and abstract geometry. Purohit had promised that he would discuss the most advanced mathematical models with Samayra.

"I think it is a fabulous idea. It might seem unreal to general people but I have full faith that you will do it." Samayra looked at the diagram which had intertwined triangles.

"I won't be able to do it alone. You are required at every step for this theory to happen."

"I am not that capable. You are counting a lot on me. I doubt if I'll be able to provide any empirical solution." Samayra bent her head backwards on the couch.

Purohit reached the other end of his living room and poured some coffee in two cups. Samayra followed him to the open kitchen and hopped over the marble slab. He gave her a cup of coffee and started explaining how that triangular projection can create 'the area of fortune'.

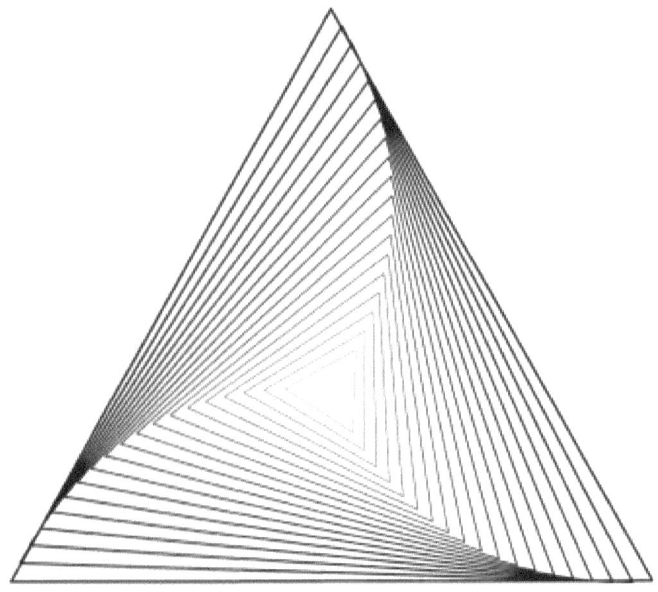

"So, the area of fortune would have the most probable events," Purohit continued.

"What sort of events would these be?"

"The events of maximum profit in a business, the events of maximum probability of finding an atomic or sub-atomic particle in an open or closed space, the events of highest level of confidence in a space of confusion, and other events of similar nature." Purohit stopped and smiled at Samayra.

Samayra was amused at the childlike innocent curiosity in Purohit's statements. His authoritative demeanor in the seminars and classrooms was contradictory to this version of him.

"Can this be extended to abstract ideas?"

"Let's try!"

"How?"

"The entire universe was nothing but a projection of humans' mind."

"So, is it not real?"

"Myth and reality go hand in hand. What our ancestors thought as a tantric practice is known as technology today. Telepathy is telephony. Magic crystals are televisions," Purohit's eyes shone as he spoke while Samayra kept looking at him in amazement. He continued, "The 'known universe' was a limitation of human senses but now it is known. The unknown Universe is the freedom of human imagination. It can be known too, and…"

"What if we do it?" Samayra exclaimed before Purohit could finish.

"With imagination, we can identify any concept."

"Even God?"

"Even love!" Purohit smiled.

"Seems unreal, but I believe you if you say so."

"The humanity is not about what we are capable of perceiving. It is about what is out there!"

'What is out there?"

"Reality!"

"What is reality?"

"It is not what people think it is. People can sense the touch, sound, smell, taste and sight, but there are things they feel."

"Things like love?"

"It is the prime mover of all events and occurrences across the Universe. It is why the heavenly bodies keep on moving in their respective orbits. It is the gravity."

"Einstein once said that gravity is not responsible for people falling in love," Samayra laughed.

"That was a smart statement, but do you realise what he actually wanted to say?"

"He tried to sound smart!"

"He would be indicating that love is so real that even gravity can't explain it. The reality is blurred in human thoughts. Even if love doesn't have a three dimensional physical shape, it is felt. It is everywhere."

They kept on talking till midnight until Samayra started feeling sleepy. Purohit showed her the way to the bedroom and lied on the couch. He looked at the 'area of fortune' again. The infinite convergences would lead him to the event where he could be happy.

He dozed off after a while.

Next morning he woke up to notice that he was covered with a blanket. It was 11 AM. He had slept longer than usual. He went to the bedroom. Samayra was not there. He checked his phone.

Sorry. Had to leave... Did not want to wake you up... Drop a text when you see this.

Good Morning!

I wish I could think like you in mathematics. The area of fortune is a fabulous concept. (Samayra replied instantly as if she had been waiting for his text)

I think you think like me.

You are just being generous. I know I don't have what is required to help you in this theory.

What if I train you?

Oh that would be great! When can we start the training?

After I return from Chandigarh...

Chandigarh?

I have to leave tomorrow as I am required there for a month.

Oh! A month is a lot.

Yes! But till then, you can educate yourself more for working on the theorems.

It is not about theorems.

Then?

Nothing! There is coffee in the thermos flask. Don't go hungry to office!

Haha! Okay!

Purohit poured out the coffee in his cup and walked to the balcony. He sipped on his coffee and watched the kids in the playground. There were families, couples, men and women. He saw an old lady struggling with her luggage. He ran downstairs and helped her. The lady blessed him. It was beautiful. He was smiling. The soothing sun of the winters, flying birds, little children and memories of last night! He realized the simplicity of life. Love brought happiness!

Samayra leaned on the boundary of her balcony. She looked around herself. There was something in her which wanted to stop Purohit. She even thought of going with him, but the college had trimesters in a week. After a while she realized she was getting dependent on her feelings about him. Her mother had grown her to be a fine independent lady. That costed her sadness at first, and then fear. What if he goes forever?

The sun was shining and the birds were singing. The children were playing, but she was scared.

Love brought fear!

∞ ∞ ∞

EVENT 7
Two Brains

Centuries ago, humanity was still to find a culture. Before humans, all others plants and animals depending on their intelligence were capable of surviving. Humans were the only organisms which understood more than survival. They developed societies and culture. Bond pairing developed for better rearing of children. Love had utility. All went well. The society became progressive. The successful evolution of humanity gave rise to culture, technology, arts and sciences.

Then, a few humans gave insights to the non-physical aspects as well. Those were the humans of future. They were the philosophers who could tell good from bad. The philosophy lost ground when more and more people got educated. The vagueness and subjectivity of philosophy seemed unreal. Another breed of intellectuals understood that whatever looks unreal in the past becomes real in the future. They built an empirical framework for all thoughts and perceptions. Hence, mathematics was born.

Mathematics is empirical philosophy!

They were the mathematicians who gave humanity new senses and directions. In the twentieth century, the mathematics developed in such a way that humanity tried to find the verifiable and publishable proofs of existence of emotions and faiths.

Purohit was a mathematician who realized this need more than others. He had a motive. He wanted to let his beloved know that feelings are real and permanent. They can go up to the extreme limits, if there were any. He wanted to prove that love transcends the apparent boundaries and established notions of humanity. Till eternity!

Samayra had made her mind against falling for Purohit. She had witnessed many examples where two people were madly in love but parted ways. It was not just the case with weak people. Even the strongest people had to part ways because of social and cultural limitations.

She replied to Purohit's texts but never initiated a conversation. She made herself busy with studies and dropped the idea of working with him. One part of her wanted to meet him. The other one stopped her. She had developed two brains inside her. One asked to be free about her feelings. The other asked to avoid any feelings. One told her that love is pure. The other told her love is a myth.

Purohit on the other hand was unknown to the fact that Samayra had her insecurities. He was in love, for the very first time, in real. He kept on devising ways to propose to Samayra about how much he loved her. He read various blogs and books on the best ways to let someone know about love. Nothing helped. Mathematics did! The concept of Infinity did!

He started working on hyperspaces[4]. He wrote theorems and functions on pages, windowpanes, walls and hands. After several iterations, he came across the greatest revelation that if there is something which can surpass infinity, then that is love. Every day he thought to himself he loved her infinitely, but after talking to her he would conclude he loved her even more. In mathematics, anything added to infinity, produces infinity.

When he tried to add infinity to the sum of infinite infinities, the result was her! She was his infinity!

---

[4] Spaces of more than three dimensions

In the third week, their conversations had reduced to formal salutations, but Purohit had patience. He waited for her birthday on January 16th. He dropped a text that he would be in Delhi from 16th to 18th.

∞ ∞ ∞

EVENT 8
Samayra's birthday

It was just another usual day in the hostel except the fact that she took exact forty seven minutes to decide on today's outfit, unlike the usual fifteen minutes. That is the only deviation her birthday brought in her everyday routine.

The dresses which were too fancy or too bland were ostracized first. Then she started screening through the rest. Some made it to the last round, some made her dubious and the rest made her question why did she ever buy them.

In the last round, they were ranked with respect to their compatibility with the footwear and accessories. All this done so far, though time consuming, did not demand so much brainstorming as deciding the final results did. She took the last twelve minutes for narrowing it down to one from amongst the two finalists. Being of her favorite color fetched one more point in favor of the pink dress and without further ado, the winner was awarded when Samayra was arrayed in it.

While on his way to Delhi, Purohit wondered whether the woman for whom he was travelling will be able to take out time to meet him. So, instead of assuming anything on his own, he texted Samayra and inquired about her plans with friends. Samayra told him that her friends were scheduled for the evening and she will be able to meet him in the afternoon.

No matter how hard she tried, their conversation told Purohit that she had been trying to adjust for him. He repented for not considering her limitations before. He texted, "I think I will have to postpone my visit because of some contingencies. Can we meet a day after?"

"I have plans for tomorrow too, but I will re-schedule. See you tomorrow then."

"Do not upset your schedules. I just thought it would be good to drop by and meet you while I am in the city. Just let me know if you are free, but don't change your plans"

"Acknowledged!"

He reached Delhi and waited thinking about her. He looked at the small velvet box, waiting to be delivered to his beloved the next day, as birthday gift.

The next day, one of her plans got cancelled the last minute. But it would have taken two hours for Purohit to reach where she was, or for her to reach where he was, or one hour for them to decide a spot in between and meet there. All in all, it would have taken one hour of travelling, two hours of meeting and one hour of travelling back. But her hostel deadlines did not allow the four hour expedition. So they could not meet that day too.

In the evening, he was communicated that he had to take an important class the following morning. The class could not be postponed even after his requests. He booked the early bus.

He informed Samayra about his preponed departure and asked whether they can meet early in the morning before him leaving. Due to time constraints of her hostel, it was decided that he will come to her dwelling and they will meet for a few minutes.

Samayra thought they will meet, exchange some formal gestures, do some small talks and he will leave.

Purohit thought she will come outside; he will capture the moment in his vivid memory, hand over her birthday gift and leave with a part of her.

5 AM

The beloved was there, well clad against the cold, wearing her pajamas and sweatshirt with a shawl draped around it. He was as stoned as he expected he will be on seeing her. It took her lifting of her eyebrows three times to bring him out of this amazement. After exchanging a few greetings, none of them knew what to say. As the onus of keeping the conversation going falls on the guys conventionally, he assumed his responsibility of striking a few jokes and suggested a walk.

She caught him observing her and felt the impulse of explaining, "I woke up late, so could not get dressed. Sorry for making you walk with me while I look like an idiot"

"You look beautiful! Innocent and fresh like a baby!"

She was confused whether it was flirting or something else. She decided to grant him some time and not be judgmental this quick. Purohit realized it was not his way of speaking. What he did next seemed weird.

"Well, I have to go. This is for you," He took out the gift.

"Oh no ... I do not take gifts." She said without looking at the gift.

"Please take it." It was just a small box. Before she could say anything, he continued, "It took me 20 days to make it."

"You made what?"

She got curious and opened it. Her childlike curiosity came to the fore, and he was missing that expression already. It was a pen drive!

"A pen drive?" She laughed.

"Mm... Hmm..."

"I think I can take it" She said and kept it in her pocket.

Purohit knew at once it would be awkward if he said anything else and decided to leave. "I think I should leave now or I will miss the bus."

They shook hands and he left, while Samayra kept observing him till he was visible. He looked back once before turning to the next street. She smiled and waved him goodbye. Samayra looked at the pen-drive and hurried inside. She entered her room and opened her laptop. Her roommate looked suspicious about the pen-drive in her hands.

"I think it is just some pen drive of songs," Samayra chuckled.

"Who gave it?" The roommate smiled sheepishly.

"A friend!" Samayra dodged the possibility of being questioned further.

This settled the inquisitiveness of the roommate and she did not show any further interests. Samayra opened her laptop and inserted the pen drive in it. It contained two files- one graph plotter and a text file which had the weirdest functions she had ever seen. This started an altogether new adrenaline rush in her. Now it was not just a gift; it was a mathematical gift. She could feel the ear to ear smile on her face when she was entering the functions one-by-one on the graph plotter. Her cheeks hurt but she could not let go off the idiotic smile.

As the graph was taking shape, her focus shifted from the graph in front of her to the guy who gifted it to her. She marveled on his knowledge, and the humility he possessed even after having some of the most coveted abilities. She thought about the childlike expressions he made that morning which is rarely worn by a man who knows this much. Now she was again at square one with respect to forming a judgement about him.

The entire screen flashed white at first. A black dot emerged at the center. As she entered more functions, many more dots emerged. The scene was no less than the aerial view of some dancers forming patterns on the dance floor. The dancers increased exponentially and so did the speed of their dance. They left behind a trail of curves and lines. The figure was finally revealed

A pair of eyes, wafer thin lips, some hair draping over a broad forehead and an ear to ear smile!

She got amused to look at her own face formed by mathematical functions. God was surely a mathematician. He must be busy in his laboratory developing new functions; functions of plants, animals, forces, nature and humans. She looked at herself and then at the box which read:

THE MATHEMATICAL PAINTING!

Maybe she was not at square one anymore. And to go further, she texted, "Can we meet?"

On his way, he stopped the cab and had tea. He got late and could not catch the bus. Coincidentally, he felt the urge to have a leisurely cup of tea only after reading her text and replying her to come to the bus stand as soon as possible. He knew it was going to have consequences on his ties with the company he worked for. But he assured himself that he could not have come sooner.

7:30 AM

Samayra reached the Interstate Bus Terminal. She found him peeping through the window of every cab that passed by. She caught him unaware. To his surprise, he was as excited to see her as he was in the morning.

"What were you looking for staring at every cab?"

"I was just looking at the number plates and trying to figure out some pattern." Being a mathematician saved him from the embarrassment. Samayra smiled. Purohit understood that he had been caught.

"Tell me you were looking for me!"

"Hmm..."

"How did you do it? How are you so good in the subject?," She blinked her eyes. Purohit didn't understand what his image was in front of her. He didn't want compliments this time. He needed an opportunity to tell that he loved her more than any possible comprehension. Was he too quick in desiring the results?

"It was never about mathematics," he said.

"What is it then?"

"That you will get to know in some time," he didn't have a politically correct answer.

"When? And more importantly, how?" Samayra was inquisitive.

"Where should we sit?"

"Anywhere is fine with me," she kept looking at him as if hooked by his hypnotism. They sat on the platform and she took out her diary. She wanted to know the mathematics. Probably feelings and mathematics do not go together.

He started explaining, "The best math students can plot any curve from their curriculum. And the best math teachers can plot any curve outside the curriculum. The mainstream mathematicians can represent any curve as a function. But the most creative mathematical artists can represent anything as a function. Also, I hope you did not see the hidden code and I still have the opportunity to present it while you are in front of me so that I can conjure your approval from the expressions on your face when you see what I am about to show you."

Mathematical Artists! That was smart, she thought.

"Which code? I have gone through all the codes in the files."

"Perfect! Open the box again."

Samayra opened the box excitedly.

"What now?" She asked.

"There is a small pocket inside the velvety covering of the inside of the lid."

"Oh there it is," she found a piece of paper.

It had another function written in some vague mathematical symbols which she could not understand. She caught his eyes anchored on her face and then roaming around her face. She felt a bit conscious. But her fascination overpowered the suspicion and he got the opportunity to explain. Purohit asked her to insert the functions from the paper. What happened next shook Samayra off her feet!

The 2D portrait of her transformed into a 3D figure!

He asked her to rotate it in any direction she wanted. It was an impeccable 3D figure of her. He was not only a great mathematician, but also a wonderful observer. He continued telling some more functions and she kept on entering diligently.

The figure extended from just face to neck and then to a perfect presentation of her collar bone, chiseled and symmetrical. She got a little doubtful about what was coming next. To her relief, he asked what she wanted to wear! She laughed out loud and he kept on looking at her. She looked as beautiful as anything can be!

"Anything you would like to see me in," she continued laughing. She felt for the very first time that she knew the guy. A respectful, eccentric and observant artist! As a mathematician, numbers were his art and as a writer, it was the words.

She took a moment to fathom the sincerity of the eyes which were taking her measurements. Things grew! More respect for him in her mind, and more love for her in his heart!

Purohit had missed his session that day. It was the first time his credibility as a trainer was questioned, but love was worth taking the risk. Next day he revived his contract and reached Chandigarh.

A month passed! Purohit felt that one month had distanced Samayra from him. His messages were either getting ignored or there were small talks. Two more months passed. He was expecting that she would tell more about how she liked the gift he had made, but she never talked about it.

The best thing about infinity is that it never ends. Every point is beginning. Purohit thought to start afresh. Two weeks later, he sent her a message…

∞ ∞ ∞

EVENT 9
The Messages

9:07 AM Hi, how are you?

(After thinking about her the whole night, he finally gathered the courage to text her)

8:49 PM I am good. What about you?

(Purohit could not dare to ask what took her this long to reply)

8:50 PM I am also good. Was just out for a walk…

8:50 PM Good.

(Purohit took it as a signal that she is busy and decided not to disturb)

8:52 PM So, what is new?

(A simple and courteous text for her, but a lifeline for him)

8:53 PM Nothing much… Just the usual… Waking up, teaching, coffee, some food and then good night… Sometimes with dreams but mostly without…

(Purohit had started being himself)

8:54 PM Wow, you just made life sound as monotonous as possible.

8:56 PM Life is the non-monotonous part of this routine which I did not mention. Developing new theorems, leisurely walk home... The few people who are always there… The list is endless.

8:58 PM You are right. Life is what happens in between the routines.

8:59 PM So, What is your life?

(Purohit thought he might have stepped out of line)

9:00 PM Ummm

(He was a little relieved)

9:02 PM I think I don't have any life. My life is the routine of this B School.

(Being an over-thinker, she took time)

9:02 PM There is got to be something?

9:03 PM Nothing

9:03 PM Friends?

9:04 PM Many, but no one can be called life.

9:04 PM Hobbies?

(Purohit was not putting efforts to converse any more. They were just going with the flow)

9:05 PM Used to do a few things back in school. But it has been ages now.

9:06 PM I got one

9:06 PM What?

9:07 PM Family?

9:07 PM You finally did get one.

9:08 PM Yay

They talked for long that day, and days after that. Samayra understood that talking to Purohit made her feel great about herself. Her second brain was becoming weak, day by day. They were at the stage where they knew things about each other like favourite color, fear of heights, food preferences, family members, sleeping routines, hostel deadlines, list of friends, ambitions, weird philosophies they have been developing since childhood, and many more.

Samayra: What is your favourite number?

(Once the girl asked the math guy)

Purohit: All prime numbers are my favourite.

Samayra: Let me guess the reason. Because they do not depend on any other number?

Purohit: Depend as if?

Samayra: Yep, numbers depend on their factors. The repetition of their factors makes them. But prime numbers are self-made. Aren't they?

Purohit: That is a nice approach I must say. So what is your favourite number?

Samayra: Number 36. Because 2 and 3 together can form all the numbers except 1… So, they have quite a lot of power. Multiplying them makes 6 and squaring 6 makes 36.

Purohit: Why multiplying and squaring?

Samayra: In order to increase the power.

Purohit: Why not squaring or cubing further?

Samayra: Well, too much power is a dangerous thing. It is imperative to have limits. ☺ ☺

They had the type of conversations which people normally could never have. They discussed about weirdest of the weird topics on earth. They had been holding all these philosophies within themselves for years, because they had no one to share it with. But now they had the listeners who could comprehend their thoughts. It was as if both of them found the person they had been looking for; with whom they could be themselves, who not only understands, but also shares the weirdest traits. They had become each other's reservoir of thoughts. They had started talking about everything worth talking happening in their lives.

Purohit: Ha ha! I want to go on a trip soon.

Samayra: I sometimes wish I was as courageous as to go on solo trips.

Purohit: You'll be. Once you go on a trip with me.

Samayra: What will you do differently on your trips?

Purohit: For starters, the destinations are different. I will not take you to hill stations or resorts. I'll take you to Aurora, to show Northern Lights.

Samayra: Where and what is that?

(Purohit sent a picture of the Northern Lights with a link)

Samayra: Wow ☺ If I go here with you, we will certainly become trip partners, as it will be the best trip ever.

Purohit: It won't remain the best after we go to Antarctica.

(He sent another link and the picture)

Samayra: Just when I thought it could not get better, it did.

Purohit: It'll get even better if we go to an unmanned island.

Samayra: Wait, isn't that risky?

(The cautious version of her resurfaced, but in a humorous way)

Purohit: What risk?

Samayra: Food, electricity, wild animals, electricity?

Purohit: We would take care of that.

Samayra: What if any ancient cannibal tribe eats us up?

Purohit: I would convince them.

Samayra: Your charm would act there too?

Purohit: Where has it worked, yet?

Samayra: In the workshops! I have seen how students fall for you. Majorly females… ☺ ☺

(Samayra felt she shouldn't have said that)

Purohit: I never noticed that.

Samayra: Well, what would we do on an unmanned island?

Purohit: Roam around for a week and then come back. We would cook food.

Samayra: You would cook. Not we…

Purohit: Okay I will

Samayra:☺ ☺ **You sure about all the things?**

Purohit: I'll think of all the contingencies beforehand and will provide for them.

Samayra: If you say it, I consider it done.

Many days and nights passed. Samayra looked up to him for motivation. Purohit was a magician for her. He had solutions to every problem of hers. More than that, he had the power to convince her that her solutions existed within her.

A few months ago, Samayra used to conclude the day she had to herself before sleeping. Now she elaborated and asked for opinions on the day she had from Purohit every night. Purohit never thought he needed expressions to communicate until now.

Purohit knew their minds when combined could do wonders and work out theorems which were unconceivable for general minds. He could do all that alone too. But it is an established fact that no matter how efficient the alpha male is, he needs an alpha female for approvals. He had found his alpha female.

But between all this, there was one thing they never talked about- Samayra's insecurities. Purohit knew they were there. But what he did not know was the reason and the consequences. Being a good cook, he knew the importance of waiting. So he chose to wait for the right time for that topic to come up.

The following one month passed in haste. He got more contracts and less time. Samayra continued with her post-graduation. But no matter how busy they were, they always had the time to talk to each other.

Suddenly she had stopped replying to any sort of communication intended by him. During this month, Purohit developed insecurities of his own. He went through all the conversations they have had, in his mind. He found many instances where he could have sounded wittier, but not a single instance he can pin point to and say, "This is where it went wrong". Whatever the reason being, he was not ready to let her go from his thoughts.

∞ ∞ ∞

EVENT 10
Love came back

*Samayra had stopped responding to all his texts, calls and mails. For Purohit, this absence of contact after the 24*7 chats they had was nothing less than the venomous snake hissing at the 99th box in the snakes and ladders game. For a week, he kept waiting for any kind of communication from her side. It looked like he had to get '6' on his die to start again. His way of looking at reality was weird. His imagination was not limited to anything, but mathematics. He could not form any strategy but wait until the number '6' came as a notification after a month, "text from Samayra".*

She had caught dengue and her family took her home. He wondered what made her forget him altogether for one month, but he did not dare to ask.

The two weeks of dengue gave her the time to reflect upon how connected they had become with the incessant exchange of texts and calls. This realization did not make her feel good. It scared her. Letting her guards down was not a Samayra thing. She knew she could not feel for him, or anyone, ever! She knew eternity did not exist when it comes to relationships. No matter how interesting it is to know new people, you either get bored of them with time or find out some characteristic of them which makes them unbearable. "If no one is going to stay forever, then why to get attached to someone" had been her agenda for life, though she never told it to anyone. There was turbulence in her inner self, but the surface was always composed, like an ocean.

She had made a shell throughout her life. She knew he was the kind of person who had the potential to take her out of it. And when she is out, all her insecurities will be exposed and secrets wide open. It was difficult to decide whether it was the medicines or just the thought of getting out of the shell that made her wobbly. It took her one month to gather the courage to reply to his texts courteously. But this is not the explanation she gave to him. Not only because she thought he wouldn't understand it, but also because he never asked for it.

Purohit told "I will be in the city tomorrow for signing the contract for one of my books on poetry."

A part of her wanted to ask him to meet her. The other wondered why the first part was being irrational! She had always been biased in favor of the latter part, so she changed the topic.

"Are you planning a proper career in poetry as well?"

"Yes!"

"What kind of poetry do you intend to publish?" She posed another question for the sake of conversation.

"About people I know."

"Do they know?"

"No."

The conversation went well and met its end. But neither of them brought up the question about their meeting the next day. Insecurity stopped the girl and abstinence from sounding pestering stopped the guy. The next day he reached Delhi and did the paper work he was supposed to. Their conversation took place at 11PM yesterday. It took 8 hours for the first part of Samayra to convince the second.

At 7 AM, she texted, "I was wondering if we could catch up today. I will be free from 1 PM."

"Great. See you then!" Purohit didn't say much but was excited, as always.

1 PM

They met at a coffee house. From her college to their families, the conversation wandered. They did not realise when they became comfortable again.

Samayra continued, "I was 8 years old. My best friend was absent that day, so I was going home alone. As any other class, there was this gang of spoilt boys in mine. They came from behind and pulled my bag. I fell on the ground but did not cry until I was home in the embrace of my mother."

"I would have thrashed the assholes who bullied you if I were there." Purohit realized he should not have said that. She did not respond and rolled her eyes.

"This was not the only time. I have been the focus of bullying quite a lot of times. What I could not figure out is the reason behind this. Was I weak or were they jealous?"

"The latter one was the reason. I can tell from your frame that you are a physically strong person. And the conversations we have had so far clearly indicate your mental strength."

"You are better when you talk mathematics," she said and laughed. Purohit wasn't sure how others talked.

"You must have been the most adorable girl in your childhood," he continued.

"I indeed was. I can recollect the memory of every other adult pulling my cheeks."

"So was I. I never knew the answers to any of the questions in the class, but my charm always saved me from the scolding," Purohit bowed down his head.

"I had this collection of ribbons for hair. I never stepped out of the house without wearing one which matched exactly to the color of my dress."

"And I had this friend without whom I never went to school."

"I can relate. I used to cry my heart out whenever I had to go to school without my elder sister. Once she did not inform our parents about her sickness. She knew if she told, I will have to go alone, though she faced the consequences later!" Samayra waved her hands.

"You are a pampered child, aren't you?"

"Yup, raised by two mothers. One is my birth mom, and other my elder sister!"

The children in them talked until it was her PG deadline. "Looks like it is the time to leave" she said.

"Can I drop you?"

"I can go on my own."

"I just want to buy some more time."

She agreed.

On the way to her hostel, Purohit thought of asking her to start working on the theory they had discussed months ago but he did not have the courage to bear a negative answer. Neither did Samayra talk about the theory, ever. So, he decided to take forward his theory of God and Love, all alone...

∞ ∞ ∞

EVENT 11
Closer

They say if someone comes back on their own, they will never leave again.

Samayra did come back. They got closer than before. The frequency of their physical meetings had increased by now. One day Samayra asked, "Why did you classify all your inventions of mathematics into seven theorems?"

"The same reason why you were sitting on the seventh seat..."

"I did not understand it."

"We think the same way!"

"How do you know that?"

"I know my brain. I know yours too, I believe. We think same!"

"How?" Samayra was visually surprised.

"Ninety percent of our thoughts are same."

"I would like to differ here. We both are different personalities." She twisted her lips in her own particular way.

"The other ten percent can contain that."

"Only ten! I do not think so."

"Eventually, you will!"

"I do agree with your opinions and theories but that doesn't mean we are same. You are way better than me in every aspect of life, knowledge and intellect."

"Would you work with me?" He could not resist the possibility of being with her, so he asked again.

"Wait, what? I thought you have already started working on it, as I was sick."

"You could have asked."

"I thought that would be too much to ask for."

"Why do you say that? Together we can accomplish what I have not been able to figure out alone in mathematics. Haven't you realized that yet?"

Purohit knew the best way to get Samayra out of her insecurities was to make her believe in her own potential. He had charted it well. Making her love herself was the requisite to make her capable of loving another being.

Samayra wanted to work, but she did not think she was the right choice. 'He could have chosen anyone. He should have chosen someone else, someone better, who could add value to his efforts'- was her trail of thoughts. She acceded neither to her under-confident thoughts nor his belief in her. She agreed to work out of her desire to learn.

Work was never work. He presented theorems as anecdotes and formulae as morals of stories. The avid liste ner got her dreams back after listening to all the transcendental tales. The reservations in her had started withering away and she contributed to his work. Her contribution awarded her more confidence in herself. The newly found composure made its own place by sidelining all the non-positive thoughts which resided in her hitherto.

Samayra was about to complete her MBA. Impromptu as he was, Purohit suggested leaving for one of the trips they had planned during the break she would get after graduation. Overcautious as she was, Samayra took a few days to sort out permissions, schedules and her own mind.

And, they went!

To one of the many places they planned for...

∞ ∞ ∞

Event 12
AURORA

November 7, 2012

Travelling together exposes each other to the deepest levels of personality, the ambitions, strengths and weaknesses, and much more. It did the same for Purohit and Samayra. On the list of places to visit, they chose Finland first. Purohit had a dream to witness Aurora and Samayra was comparatively free.

They landed in Finland at 0530 hours. The trip planners had arranged a car which was supposed to drive them to the Ice Resort. The driver was a young man who told them about the things-to-do and not-to-do at Arctic Circle.

"You are from India?" He asked in his crisp Finnish accent.

"Yes," Purohit answered as Samayra was busy looking at the snowy countryside.

"The chances are low but beware of the Polar Bears," the man said and adjusted his rearview mirror.

"I have heard about them. They are the only animals which actively prey on humans," Purohit urged.

"Exactly!"

The countryside was small but looked vast as the flora was rare. The ground was swollen and the grass was withered. The arctic dogs were plump and looked interested as the human intrusion was less. There were occasional snow showers, and children played around on the snow.

"How far from here?" Purohit asked.

"A mile or two!"

They reached the Ice Resort at 0730 hours. The entire resort was a few acres of hard white ice, with igloos scattered at distances of a few feet. It was a perfect paradise for families and couples. They checked-in to their igloo and bid the young driver goodbye. Their igloo was a fifteen feet wide hemisphere build with perfect ice blocks and determination of the architects at the Ice Resort in the city of Rovaniemi. It had a circular bed tucked in milk white bed sheets. The floor was wooden and covered with thermal insulators. There were frames of tropical polar bear, reindeers and Eskimos.

Samayra googled out things about Rovaniemi. There were activities like Ice Skiing, Ice Fishing, Snowshore Adventure and of course the Arctic Lights. They still had twelve hours for witnessing the Aurora[5].

"Where should we go first?" Samayra asked looking at her phone.

"Let's sleep for a while. Experiencing jetlag, aren't you?" Purohit yawned as he lay still in the bed.

"I am excited about being here. No sleep, nothing!" She looked out of the window. The weather was dry and cold. She looked back at Purohit and frowned. He got up without further drama.

The myth about God and his abilities become a reality on the North Pole. All the five elements become the raw material for one of the most prominent magic shows naturally possible on our planet. The clouds hung low like crystalline ice flakes on the altar of the horizon like the dewy eyelids of a painter's muse. The painter picked up the densest brush and extended the eyelids in a dry stroke. He just did not stop at this. He sprayed the last

---

[5] Aurora Borealis or Arctic Lights is a natural phenomenon where there is a light display in the sky caused due to disturbances by solar winds.

remnants of his palette and painted the entire sky in grey-green-crimson hue.

Samayra had only imagined about this fantasy with Purohit, but now they were witnessing it, from the small window of their igloo. Samayra could not hold her curiosity and herself within the ice structure. She stepped out. Purohit followed. Both of them stopped near the door itself to let the beauty assimilate in them. None of them spoke anything for a few minutes. They just stood with their eyes set on the sky holding the expression of exclamation intact on their faces. Samayra took his hand in hers. She could not take this overwhelming experience alone.

"It looks like a dream," Samayra mumbled.

Purohit kept his arm around her shoulder and they walked out in the open. The ice contained their footsteps, leaving a trail behind, of togetherness. They looked like two silhouettes standing close as one single entity in the backdrop of a bluish-white igloo and icefield, covered by the largest painting up in the sky. They inspired the scenes of romanticist poems and fantasies.

"Can you imagine this after we are gone?" Purohit spoke softly in her ears.

"Gone? Where?"

"Back to where we belong..."

"We belong here, Purohit," Samayra said and hugged him. It was the first time Purohit could feel her heartbeats. Her softness against his chest! Her shivering lips against his neck! He could stay still like that for his entire life.

And, he laid still!

"You would never go anywhere," Samayra hugged him tight.

"I won't..." He hugged her back.

That was the night when it got etched on stone that they belonged to each other. Nothing would keep them apart!

For the next few days, they explored every adventure activity in Finland. Purohit realized that Samayra loved adventure. Samayra realized she was most natural with Purohit. She felt lucky to have such a 'friend, mentor and guide'. Love never developed in her. She was yet to know the feeling. In all possibilities, feeling love is easy, but understanding it is difficult. With every excursion, they came close and developed likelihood for each other.

∞ ∞ ∞

Event 13
Forever

"Let's go to other places you planned for, soon," Samayra said.

"Great, but why so soon?," Purohit asked.

"Life is weird," she said.

It was more than a week since they were back from the trip but they were still cherishing it under the moon with their eyes closed.

"I know it is, but I wonder what makes you say that out of nowhere." Purohit said while counting the stars.

"Just when you think it is just a simple dream you have to live and do things which makes you happy, something drives you back into the reality and reminds you of the externalities," she continued her monologue and could not pay attention to what he said.

"Dreams are what we see, and we are the people who can realise them."

"Like what dreams, Purohit?" Samayra came close and rested on his shoulder.

"The dreams which we have been seeing from last two years. The dreams of working together…"

"Being together," she smiled and adjusted his curls which waved in sync with the cool breeze.

"Travelling together," Purohit chuckled.

"The unmanned island is still left."

"Let's go now!"

"You got to cook food, remember that?"

"Yes, I do, madam," Purohit bowed.

"I have recently realized that nerds can be cute," she said and pulled his cheeks.

"People have said I have got a face which can look cute to my mother only," Purohit remarked.

"Nerds have a sense of humor too," she said and Purohit laughed.

"You can look cute to your future wife as well," Samayra didn't hold her back and hugged him. Purohit imagined the aurora building up in his mind. Stars were shooting. Comets were flying leaving behind a trail which morphed to the shape of infinity. He cajoled all the waves, all the aesthetics, all the poetry ever written, and his beloved.

"Do you believe in God?" Samayra lips trembled.

"In my pursuit to find the expressions of love, I think I will find the expression of God," Purohit was confident, more than ever. He had been trying to play God, all this while. He had created conditions to let Samayra know that love exists.

Probably God too, existed!

And if he did, he too manages the world the way Purohit was managing the events; the events which can brighten 'the area of fortune' in the most glorious ways. He had planned the events which would have converged to one simple truth- they were made for each other. They were the counterparts. They were the soulmates. A scene where they would depart would never be imagined, written, expressed, painted or played. It would never be a possibility!

"How close are you to him?" Samayra sounded dreamy. Her voice was shivering. Purohit lifted her chin. She was sobbing. Her eyes were wet.

"What happened?" He cupped her face in his palms.

"My parents are marrying me off," she said. That was beyond belief. The beautiful moonlit night became dreadful. The stars that he was counting a minute ago stopped twinkling. He could sense a wave in his stomach which rose up to his mouth and inundated his nostrils. He felt dizzy. He took hold of the balcony. "But..." He did not know how to respond and she was not in a situation to notice his response.

She continued, "I do not want to get married. But I do realize that in the real world, my parents have the right to take decisions for me. Why shouldn't they? But why are they doing this?" Her monologue had stopped making sense and her only audience was not listening. She finally stopped and looked at him for consolation. She didn't know he was in a worse state than her. He had never been the ad-lib kind. He always thought before saying.

Here, there were no thoughts, and hence, no words!

"Have you met the guy?" He asked after a while. His voice shivered too.

"I will meet him tomorrow."

"Meet him and tell me if you like him."

"Hmm!"

They didn't speak anything for a while.

"I will drive you to your hostel," Purohit offered.

While coming back, Purohit's face had grown hard. The fifteen minutes passed like eons. His muscles had gone stiff. The nose couldn't feel air. Throat was dry and feet were numb. Suddenly everything blurred. There was moisture everywhere.

He stopped his car and touched his eyes. They were drenched. He opened the gate and came out. There was no one around. A few dogs were barking at a distance. He walked to the middle of the road. Upwards was a dark sky; downwards was a barren road. He felt extreme solitude; death of ambitions, absence of vitality, failure of the world, all at once. His hands automatically moved to his ears. He pressed them hard. As hard as he could, and cried. All the voices which were left inside him were let out that night.

Samayra was not sure about what was going on in her life. The guy her parents had chosen was an eligible bachelor. *Handsome, rich and of same community! Samayra was all fine with it and texted Purohit about him. Purohit didn't respond. The WhatsApp messages didn't deliver. Two days later, she could see blue ticks on all of her messages, but there was no reply. She couldn't meet him the next day as her meeting with the prospective partner was arranged.*

Purohit on the other hand drowned in a sense of self-doubt and disapproval.

He planned to leave, forever!

∞ ∞ ∞

EVENT 14
Along came the way...

Along is a district sandwiched between the borders of India and China. The people in Along are generally welcoming of everyone because they don't yet know where India ceases and China starts to exist. They lie in a geographical transcendence which very well shows in their culture, language and attire. Purohit chose the place as his hideout because of many reasons. It offered solitude as well as human touch. A loner (if he was one) is after all a human, a social animal. Even if they don't require a society for solutions, they require it for approvals. Purohit was a human too, apart from the general notions of Samayra. Other notions were not that important, at least for him. He felt the need of having approvals (and solutions) like everyone else.

The trip to Along was a long one; flight from Delhi to Bagdogra and then a chopper trailing across the dense and rough forests of Assam and Arunachal Pradesh. It sounds exotic for a person filled with wanderlust, but for him it was an escape; from memories, friends, society, ambitions and apprehensions. The only thing he couldn't lose was hope and love. He hoped that the sun which set in Chandigarh, would rise again in Along. His equations of love would finally be solved.

Tantra Adventures, a travel agency had arranged a resourceful man from Along, who would help Purohit in settling down. After a long hunt for a place to stay, he finally settled for a hut uphill. His abode was not just a regular hut. It was surrounded by the presence of bamboo shrubs, creepers, blossom-laden trees and the munificence of fresh and cool breeze traversing through snow like cascade and Himalayan herbs. The boundary of hut was marked by bougainvillea shrubs. At the backyard, there was a kitchen garden adorned by the egg-fruits, tomatoes, peaches and cherries. The house-keeper had installed a fireplace because the climate was majorly cold and the mornings were foggy.

Purohit looked around his new home and decided to stay. It was the perfect blend of melancholy and harmony; a perfect place to theorize and prove his equations of love. The housekeeper with his nine year old kid took his leave and offered to visit every morning for domestic help.

10 PM

The valley echoed with growling hyenas, stridulating crickets, purring felines, barking hounds and rustling leaves. Purohit looked out of his window to realize that fog was descending on the widespread flora; the white smoky tinge on black silhouettes of green trees. It was something he had only dreamt about. He thought about the sage and a smile ran through his lips. He took out black paint and painted the insides of hut, the walls, the floor, the roof, the attic and the cellar. There is a thing about black. It is not a visual but the absence of all visuals. It is a sensation where the edges of physical and metaphysical realms cease to exist. The corner of the walls, the vertices of the attic, the center of the floor and the epicenter of his creativity were all invisible! All was black!

He realized he was a part of it when he closed his eyes in anticipation of the only white he could remember- her white dress.

7 AM

Knock! Knock!

He heard the faint sounds in numbness as if someone was coming in through the wormhole. He found himself lost in the absorption of blackness. He could not comprehend if his eyes were open or closed.

Knock! Knock!

The only way he could reach the door was by following the sound. Drowsy and numb, he trod his way to the door. It was the housekeeper and his son.

"Good Morning Sir," both said in unison.

"Mornin...'"

They were bamboozled to look at the walls and floors.

"Is everything alright?"

The housekeeper was a man in late thirties. His hairs were long and straight. His skin was pale and devoid of any expression except stress and worry. The young kid was a miniature of his father, but he had a happier face, probably due to his age.

"Yes, alright!"

The young kid ran across the room and found an interesting artefact created by Purohit near one of the walls. It was a brick-and-mortar assembly of a complex structure.

"Do you know what is it?" Purohit asked while the kid kept on looking at the figure in amazement.

"Cube," he chuckled.

"Tetrahedron," Purohit pronounced.

The kid mumbled the name and his lips twisted. The housekeeper and Purohit laughed.

"Which standard are you in?" Purohit picked the cup from the housekeeper and sipped on the tea.

The kid didn't answer and looked at his father.

"He doesn't go to school, Sir."

Purohit didn't ask the reason as he knew that the desire of education was still a problem in India.

"I will train him," Purohit said.

They helped him with the chores and settling that day and every other day after that.

The boy, Sonu, had a major incentive to stay at Purohit's house. Purohit was introducing him to a world he had not even dreamed of yet; the world of education. He was intrigued about it not because he imagined at as a prettier place. Along was at the zenith of beauty and nothing could be prettier than that even in his imaginations. He grew interested because it was a world of awareness. He thought everyone there must know about everyone and everything and he was living his life in this out house of oblivion.

Purohit introduced him not only to the outside, but also to the insides. He told him everything about himself. Where he came from, how he was raised, how meeting a few people changed his life and how hard it was to leave them and come all the way here. He did not only teach "who Purohit is", but also "who Sonu is" and "who Sonu would be in the future". The part of "who Sonu should be" was inferred by Sonu himself whenever he looked at Purohit.

It had become a routine for Purohit to start his research every time with new conditions and assumptions in mind. Every other iteration would produce a condition which would disprove the initial steps. In simple terms the equation proved itself to be unsolved, and all the assumptions seemed flawed. Was it one of those hypotheses which never become theorems? The progress up to now looked superfluous.

Love doesn't go alone. Something had died in him, which was not coming back to life again. He was trying hard, wo[rking day and nights, ignoring sleep and food. Nothing was working! He could feel the nights getting darker, days getting hazier, and the paint on his walls getting blacker.

One day he fell in a pit of confusion and felt that everything around him was nothing but just a myth. He started noticing things around him. He could not see the dew drops on the blades of grass anymore. The butterflies were no more iridescent. The brooks stopped flowing. The winds were still. The natural sounds were sullen. The birds no more sang. The glowworms didn't glow. The blossoms had withered. The inspiration was gone. The dream was lost. The leaves on the trees fell for never coming back. The sage was pale!

This happened with him again and again. Every year was a déjà vu, which occurred for four more times!

∞ ∞ ∞

EVENT 15
Infinity at its zero!

One fine night, at two in the morning, three people noticed a bright star, out of a full alabaster moonlit night. A few comets flew randomly and brightened the north. Something in them reminded the star was a symbol, an insignia of hope! They packed the most beautiful gift for the most beautiful procession.[6]

Love for Hope! Hope for Love!!

A hope which would change the world! The oriental notions of darkness were about to be over. All recited a song that echoed through the centuries, ancient, medieval and modern. It was the song which everyone can listen to, playing inside their souls, beneath the brine of biggest oceans, on the top of the whitest peaks, inside the shells and conches!

The modern mathematics talks about chaos, uncertainty, Brownian motion; about being, and not being; about proofs, results of empirical and verifiable nature. In a world so full of possibilities and variance, quantifying the unquantifiable emotion of love was a subjective reality, occurring at a point which is better called as Infinity!

'Infinity' was 'Samayra' now! The once lively girl was a serious woman. From the tight hair bun to the impeccably ironed drapes of her sari, everything communicated sophistication. She emanated seriousness and intensity, just the way her profession demanded. She was running an NGO working in the field of elementary education across India and South East Asia. Her work was

---

[6] The legend says that Magi is the collective term for the three kings of Orient who travelled with gifts at the birth of Jesus.

to make association with government agencies and international organizations, for funding and support.

After Purohit had left four years ago, Samayra lost hold of reality for a few months, cancelling her engagement and deciding never to get married or involved with anyone, ~~except.~~ Then she had started searching for Purohit, digging in all the companies and tie-ups he had been a part of. No possible contact, E-Mail ID or address was spared. She even contacted all the trip advisors if anyone called Purohit Khantwal had/would planned/plan a trip with them. Nothing worked. Her parents, friends and colleagues asked her to start meeting new people and mix up with society. They planned get-togethers, parties and meetings, but she would never go. Everyone around her had different versions for her love for Purohit. Even she did not know the reality.

She did not understand the reason for Purohit's leave. Neither did she know what made her so uncomfortable with his absence. Thriving to know about his whereabouts was not her perusal of her feelings for him, but the quest of knowing what her feelings were.

Whatever it was, now Samayra was used to being unsure, even after trying. It had become her natural state of mind. She couldn't know if she was happy or sad. She found solace in teaching the underprivileged, and was probably waiting for a miracle to happen. It was just that she didn't believe in miracles. It was Purohit who did! He could make them happen! He was among the founders of mathematics, and she was among the patrons. That was the only difference between them. Purohit failed in making her realize that only patrons can be creators, for everything, let alone mathematics.

Both were happy once, in similar way. Both were sad now, in their own ways.

One was disbelieving! Other was inquisitive!!

Epilogue

The wormhole opened...

The legend of Purohit and Samayra had a weird beginning and a weirder ending.

It took Samayra another three years to believe Purohit won't be back. When that happened she locked herself inside a room for a week, to realize the extreme limits of solitude. There was no sound, no light, no people...

She never told about the experience to anyone, and no one questioned. She just became headstrong and not-so-confused. She thought of letting Purohit go out of her memories, step-by-step. She opened his poems and read them. She took out pictures from their trips.

Once while cleaning the house, she found the pen drive. The mathematical paintings flashed before her eyes. She smiled. She took out her laptop and inserted the pen-drive. The nostalgia inundated her senses. She could see the functions and the curve plotters- 2 D and 3 D. She decided to plot herself again, one final time. She clicked on the text file, and to her surprise, a pop up appeared.

Are you connected to the Internet?
Yes!

A series of functions downloaded. Samayra was shocked. She felt the need to sit down. She copied all the functions and closed the text file. She opened the folder containing the curve plotters. That was beyond belief. A new icon was formed.

Multidimensional Curve Plotter...

Samayra copied the functions there, and waited for the graph to plot.

Loading...

A network of branches was formed which extended to random directions and dimensions. After a while the graphs looked like a tesseract and there was one door made of grayscale wire-mesh. Samayra moved inside the door and its width was infinitely converging towards the other end. Along the width there were wire-mesh windows each containing a three dimensional image of her time with Purohit. She maneuvered across the **infinite** gallery to reach another door with a board which read The Equation of Love. She got goosebumps!

She opened the door and reached the hallway through which he walked seven years ago. She recalled that she was standing near the seventh pillar on the left. She dragged the pointer to the seventh pillar. She could see a wire-mesh outline of herself, with the head glowing. As she moved closer she could see herself in full color. It looked like she met herself for the first time. She moved ahead and to her surprise, she walked inside her own body. It was hyper-dimension! The functions had made a three-dimensional reality for her mind to comprehend what was no more subjective!

After crossing layers of flesh, muscle and bones, she tried to move upwards. She reached her brain. Every convolution was an infinite tube. She walked through each one of them. There were windows with weird looking artefacts of higher dimensions. On every window, there were numbers.

1, 2, 3...

She looked at all the artefacts and recalled what Purohit had once said.

All the intangible aspects are actually objects of higher dimensions. Fear, pain, passion, confidence, strength, bonding, and most importantly love...

She ran across all the tubes of her own brain and counted till 89. That was weird. She took a glass of water, and moved outside of her body. At one corner Purohit was standing and she moved near him. His brain was glowing as well. His wire-mesh structure soon became the full him, confident and brooding with energy. She moved inside him and reached his brain and there were similar tubes with similar artefacts. She counted every number and her heart skipped 89 beats. The 90th was glowing at the point of infinite convergence inside his brain. She moved closer, fearing the unknown, or fearing the reality. The weird artefact looked like a giant amoeba which could shift shapes. A message appeared:

Do you want to see the curve for the ninetieth similarity?

Yes!

The amoeba transformed to her own image!!

She was the 90th window of his brain.

She moved out of his body and entered her body again, and searched for ninetieth window in desperation. A message popped up:

Are you still confused?

No!

The ninetieth window appeared and the shape shifting amoeba transformed into Purohit. This challenged all her notions that the other ten were never there, and she fainted...

Back at Along, Purohit opened his laptop and was notified that his files have been received. Purohit shut down his laptop, took out his bag and packed his stuff.

He called the Tantra Adventures again.

"Book my tickets."

"To?"

"The place I always belonged to..."

∞ ∞ ∞
He was now ready...
For the finite journey called 'life'

...with countless possibilities
Like Infinity...
∞ ∞ ∞

Upcoming Books by same authors

brahmaganita v 1.0

Mathematical Treatise
Launch Date: March 7, 2020

THE BULLET THAT ENDED OPERATION BLUESTAR

Historical and Political Thriller
Launch Date: April 9, 2020

BIG BLACK BOOK

Aptitude Preparation
Launch Date: June, 2020